WITHDRAWN

THE WAY
HOME

NAN PARSON ROSSITER

Dutton Children's Books • New York

Library of Congress Cataloging-in-Publication Data

Rossiter, Nan Parson.
The way home / by Nan Parson Rossiter.—1st ed.
p.   cm.
Summary: Late in October, Samuel and his father rescue an injured Canadian goose
and nurse her back to health on their farm, hoping that she will be able
to fly south with her mate and that they will return in the spring.
ISBN 0-525-45767-4 (hc)
[1. Canada goose—Fiction. 2. Geese—Fiction. 3. Farm life—Fiction.] I. Title.
PZ7.R72223Way   1999   [Fic]—dc21   98-54194   CIP   AC

Published in the United States 1999 by Dutton Children's Books,
a division of Penguin Putnam Books for Young Readers
345 Hudson Street, New York, New York 10014
http://www.penguinputnam.com/yreaders/index.htm
Designed by Richard Amari
Printed in Hong Kong
First Edition
1 3 5 7 9 10 8 6 4 2

In his hand is the life of every living thing and the breath of all mankind.

JOB 12:10 RSV

For Bruce, my Spruce Goose

It was late in the October afternoon when Samuel and his father finished the day's chores at the farm and set out for a walk with Ben, their yellow Lab. The sun was already behind the hills, but they had just enough time to walk around the pond before it got dark.

Dry leaves scurried across the road, chasing one another before they hid in the tall grass. Ben raced ahead, nose down, taking in every scent.

As they reached the path that wandered down to the pond, Ben stopped and stood perfectly still, with his head lowered. In a cluster of faded blue chicory flowers lay a small Canada goose. Her bright black eyes were locked onto Ben's, daring him to come closer. "Dad! Look over there!" Samuel cried excitedly.

Samuel's father gave a low whistle. "Come here, Ben. Leave that goose alone," he called softly. Ben turned away from her reluctantly and plodded over to where Samuel's father stood. Samuel held on to Ben's collar while his father moved slowly toward the

goose. She hissed loudly but made no attempt to stand up.

"What's wrong with her?" Samuel whispered urgently. "Is she hurt?"

Samuel's father knelt down next to the little goose. She didn't try to nip him with her sharp beak. She seemed to know that she needed help. Samuel's father could see that the goose was tangled in a fishing line. It was wrapped around her left wing and foot. Her struggles had made the knots in the line grow tighter. Now her wing stuck out awkwardly from her body. Her

small webbed foot was bruised and swollen where the line pinched it.

It had been a few days since Samuel and his father had heard the haunting calls of the geese overhead as they flew southward in their arrow-shaped formation to a warmer climate. This little goose must have been left behind. The lakes and ponds would soon be frozen. Samuel knew that the goose would starve without water to drink and tender plants to eat.

"We've got to help her, Dad," said Samuel. "Can you pick her up?"

"She's in pretty rough shape, pal," his father said.

"We can't just leave her here," said Samuel firmly.

"I'll give it a try. Hold on tight to Ben," said Samuel's father. He gently held the goose's neck and lifted her body up with his other hand. She was trembling. In a soothing voice, he told her that everything would be all right. Samuel hoped it was true.

"Wait! There's another goose over there," Samuel whispered, pointing behind them. Samuel's father stood up carefully and turned around. A large gander was watching them from a grove of spruce trees.

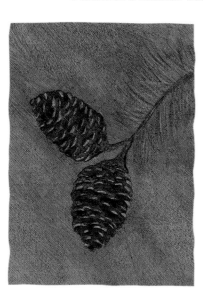

"Do you think it's the little goose's mate?" asked Samuel.

"Could be," his father answered. "Canada geese are very loyal. They pair up and stay together their whole lives. The only time they'll look for a new mate is if one dies."

"We *can't* let her die," said Samuel. As he said this, the gander waddled closer to them, honking loudly with each step.

When they reached the farmhouse, Samuel's father carried the goose inside and gently set her down on an old blanket. Then he clipped the knotted fishing line with a pair of scissors. "Someone just left this line lying around," he muttered angrily. "People can be so careless! But I don't think her wing is broken. She can still move it a little. Looks like she just strained some muscles when she tried to wriggle free."

Samuel could hear the gander honking mournfully outside in the farmyard. He opened the door so the two geese could see each other. The gander stood nearby, calling to his mate in a melancholy voice, but he wouldn't go inside.

Samuel knelt down beside the blanket. He stroked the goose's soft feathers for a little while, then got up to help his father mix warm milk and mashed oats together. Samuel set a bowl of water by the goose's head, and she drank thirstily. But when he set the food down in front of her, she turned her head away.

After supper, Samuel tried again to get the gander to come inside the house, but he refused to move closer. Samuel closed the door. "Good night, little goose," he whispered. "Sleep tight." He switched off the light and climbed the stairs to his room. He fell asleep to the sound of the gander's lonely honking.

The first thing Samuel heard the next morning was the gander's worried serenade. Samuel hurried downstairs to check on the goose. She was still lying on the blanket, but she lifted her head when he came into the room. Since his father was already outside feeding the chickens, Samuel mixed the oat mash with milk by himself. Then he carried the bowl carefully across the room and set it down in front of the little goose. She pushed her beak into it and began gobbling the food. "Wow! You must be feeling better!" Samuel watched the goose with satisfaction.

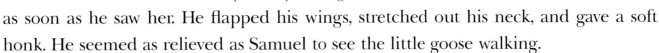

When Samuel opened the door, the goose suddenly struggled to her feet. "Look at you!" cried Samuel. "You must be feeling *lots* better!" The goose glanced back at him and blinked. Then she hobbled outside very slowly. The gander rushed over as soon as he saw her. He flapped his wings, stretched out his neck, and gave a soft honk. He seemed as relieved as Samuel to see the little goose walking.

Samuel's father came out of the barn and looked at the two geese. "Looks like she might make it, son!" he called across the farmyard.

"I *know* she's going to make it," Samuel called back. "She ate like a hog this morning!"

Samuel wanted to spend the whole day watching the goose. There was something so special about her—the funny little noises she made in her throat, the graceful way she preened her feathers. Most of the time, she lay quietly under the tractor. Once in a while she got up to drink from the water trough or nibble the grain scattered near

the barn. Samuel and his father checked on her between chores. The gander kept a close eye on them, too. Whenever Ben moved close to the little goose, the gander chased after him, wings outspread, honking and nipping at his heels. He made it very clear that he would protect his mate no matter what. Samuel laughed at the gander, but he understood the feeling of wanting to keep the little goose safe.

"Looks like these two are going to be here for a while," said Samuel's father. "Have you thought of any good names for them?"

Samuel decided to call the little goose Chicory, since they had found her in a patch of the delicate blue flowers. "And I think I'll call you Spruce Goose," he said to the gander, remembering how he'd hidden in the shadow of the spruce trees.

By the time Samuel was done with his chores for the day, Chicory was able to tuck her wing closer to her body, but it still stuck out at an odd angle. She didn't try to use it at all. Samuel worried about where the geese would sleep. He knew that Chicory would be no match for a hungry fox, even with Spruce Goose there to protect her. Suddenly he had an idea. Samuel

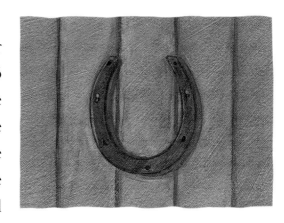

ran into the farmhouse and mixed together more oat mash. He carried the bowl outside and set it down just inside the barn. When Chicory smelled the warm food, she limped toward it, with Spruce Goose waddling just behind her. "Good night. Sleep tight," said Samuel softly as he closed and latched the barn door. "You'll be safe in there."

When Samuel opened the barn door the next morning, Chicory and Spruce Goose waddled out of the barn together, honking noisily. They ate their food hungrily while Samuel filled the trough with fresh water.

Over the next week, the geese became part of the daily routine on the farm. They spent most of the day lying in the sun or exploring new parts of the barnyard. Samuel never let them very far out of his sight.

By the second week, Chicory's wing looked normal again, and she opened it out often to exercise it. By the beginning of the third week, her wing seemed strong and healthy.

Late one afternoon while Samuel was helping his father sweep out the barn, he heard the two geese honking. He rushed outside to see what was going on. "Dad! Come quick!" Samuel yelled. His father ran out of the barn just in time to see Chicory and Spruce Goose lift off together.

"Look at them go!" Samuel's father cried. The geese circled the farm again and again, honking to each other.

Chicory looked beautiful, dipping and stretching her wings in the wind. Samuel followed her progress with his eyes. This was the moment he had been hoping for. But now that it was here, Samuel didn't know how to feel. He was excited and proud, lonely and sad all at the same time.

At dusk, the two geese drifted to a landing beside the tractor. Chicory strutted and stretched out her neck toward Samuel. "Silly old goose," Samuel said. He opened the

barn door and watched the geese settle down in the warm straw. "Good night. Sleep tight," he said softly. His feet felt heavy as he walked toward the house.

It took a very long time for Samuel to fall asleep that night. When he finally did, he dreamed that he was flying south with the geese. He could feel the wind tugging at his clothes and lifting him higher and higher above the farm.

The next morning dawned clear and crisp. The sky, which for days had been full of threatening snow clouds, was now bright blue. It was a perfect day for a hike... or, Samuel suddenly realized, a long flight. He quickly mixed food for the geese and carried the steaming bowl out to the barn. His father was lugging a heavy sack of grain through the big doors. Samuel followed him in. The stall where Chicory and Spruce Goose usually slept was empty.

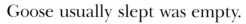

"Where are they?" Samuel asked. "Are they gone already?"

"Looks like it," his father answered, turning to pour some grain into the feed trough for the cows. "It won't be the same around here without them, will it?"

"No," said Samuel, kicking at the straw on the barn floor.

"You should be really proud that you helped them get on their way," his father said.

Samuel didn't look up. "I wanted to say good-bye. They could have waited a little longer."

"They have a long way to go—I'm sure they just wanted to get an early start," his father said. When he saw the tears in Samuel's eyes, he put the feed bag down and wrapped him in a tight hug. "I'm going to miss them too, son."

Suddenly the morning filled with loud honking. Samuel and his father hurried outside and looked toward the pond. Chicory and Spruce Goose flew low over the farm-yard and circled once overhead. Then they lifted higher and turned southward.

Waving wildly and smiling through his tears, Samuel watched the geese until they were out of sight. "Good-bye, Chicory! Good-bye, Spruce Goose! Good luck!" he yelled

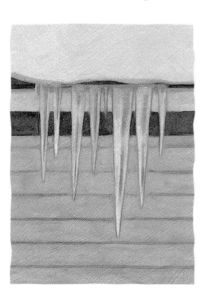

as loud as he could. When Samuel could no longer hear their calls, he followed his father back into the barn.

That night a thick layer of snow covered the farm. Icicles sparkled on the eaves of the house. Even though he missed the geese, Samuel was glad to know that they were on their way to a warmer place.

Through the long winter, Samuel and his father often talked about the two wild geese, wondering if they had made it to their southern haven and found their flock. Samuel drew pictures of them until the refrigerator was covered with soaring geese.

"Do you think we'll ever see them again, Dad?"

"I don't know. Geese come back to the same place spring after spring. Maybe they'll remember us," his father answered, gazing out the window at the snow-covered farmyard.

Samuel thought about when the flock had come to the pond last spring. He loved to watch them skid and splash along the surface of the water as they swooped in for a landing. The geese had made nests and laid their large white eggs in the tall reeds at the edge of the pond. Samuel knew that some of the older pairs even used the same nests year after year. Samuel pictured Chicory in his mind, splashing in a warm lake somewhere far away from the snow and ice. But what if she and Spruce Goose had never made it? Samuel tried to push away his worried thoughts.

After weeks of snowstorms and freezing temperatures, the earth began to show signs of spring. Crocuses popped up through patches of snow. The air smelled fresh and sweet. Samuel and his father were very busy with chores around the farm. They planted peas, carrots, and spinach in the kitchen garden. They raked the leaves and old straw out of the farmyard. There was hardly any time for Ben's daily walk around the pond, but he didn't seem to mind. He was content to lie in the soft new grass and soak up the warmth of the sun.

One morning Samuel heard Ben barking excitedly. "What is it, boy? What do you hear?" Samuel asked, trying to calm him down.

Then, along with the barking, Samuel heard another sound, faintly at first.

Ben galloped out of the farmyard, and Samuel ran hard to catch up with him. Ben skidded to a halt. Samuel could hardly believe his eyes: There was Spruce Goose, strutting up the path from the pond. Parading behind him were five fuzzy, noisy goslings. And last of all came their proud mama, Chicory, honking and stretching out her long, graceful neck.

"You made it!" cried Samuel. "Welcome home!" Then he ran back to the barn to tell his father the good news.

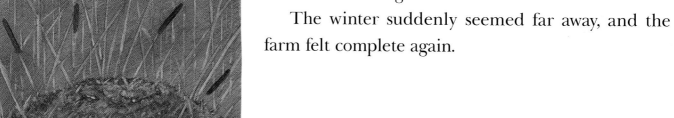

The winter suddenly seemed far away, and the farm felt complete again.